a voice
like a hand

shaking me

out of sleep

deep

raw

young

male

Has he come back?

ALSO BY A. M. JENKINS

A.M. JENKINS

BEATING HEART

An Imprint of HarperCollins*Publishers*

Beating Heart: A Ghost Story

Copyright © 2006 by A. M. Jenkins

Library of Congress Cataloging-in-Publication Data

Jenkins, A. M. (Amanda McRaney)

  Beating heart : a ghost story / by A. M. Jenkins.—1st ed.

    p.   cm.

  Summary: Following his parents' divorce, seventeen-year-old Evan moves with his mother and sister into an old house where the spirit of a teenager who died there awakens and mistakes him for her long-departed lover.

  ISBN 978-0-06-054609-0

  [1. Ghosts—Fiction. 2. Haunted houses—Fiction. 3. Divorce—Fiction. 4. Moving, Household—Fiction.] I. Title.

PZ7.J4125Bea 2006   2005005071

[Fic]—dc22   CIP   AC

Typography by Karin Paprocki

09 10 11 12 13 LP/CW

10 9 8 7 6 5 4 3 2 1

❖   First paperback edition

Dedicated to the memory of
Bill Morris, a man with a heart
for both books and people

ACKNOWLEDGMENTS

I owe a debt of gratitude to the following people for their critiques, common sense, and/or commiseration: Lisa Firke, Chris Ford, Amy Butler Greenfield, Shirley Harazin, Cindy Lord, Martha Moore, Anne Marie Pace, Mary Pearson, Diane Roberts, Nancy Werlin, Laura Wiess, and Melissa Wyatt. Many thanks are also due to Steve Malk and Alix Reid, and especially to Anne Hoppe for her guidance in selecting and shaping the proper pieces, and getting them nailed into place.

BEATING
HEART

I doze
    content

this house

    is mine—

        beloved, familiar.

I am

    this house

the air is still

      an unopened present

untouched

        safe

wind rakes the roof tiles

plucks at the eaves

drops of rain
      break
      against the windowpane

            run
            formless

            down

            the

            glass

scattered dreams

of

people

scurrying

about the house

flecks of dust

float in sunlight

warm,

silent

light makes its way
            under
            the
            wide
porch roof

                    softened, blurred
                    gentled

                    by its journey

the wide hall
        is flanked by rooms
washed in silence

voices
turn to echoes,
            fading away
                  before
they can
become
            words

pleasant

unpinned

the rooms and I

drifting

we have no names

This house

is mine

and

I am

its beating heart.

*E*van is not impressed when he first walks into the house. There is no electricity; the only light comes in through the open door, and through the windows in rooms on either side of the hall. The wallpaper has been eaten away in patches. The wooden floors are gritty underfoot. Ivy has actually curled its way over a windowsill into the house, through one unevenly fitted sash. At the end of the hall, a wide staircase rises and seems to disappear into gloom.

Evan's mother is brimming with quiet satisfaction, and Libby, who is five, prances with excitement. But Evan feels skeptical. "This is it?" he asks.

Mom nods. "Isn't it beautiful?"

Libby skips toward the stairs, craning her neck to look up. She runs her fingers along the dusty scrolled banister. "It's like a castle!"

Mom smiles, then turns to Evan. "What do you

think?" she asks him.

Evan looks around at the dirt, the dust, the whole derelict, falling-apart thing. "You want me to be honest?"

"Of course."

"I think it's the biggest dump I've ever seen."

Mom shakes her head. "You're not looking at the potential."

"Mom." Evan can't believe she's oblivious to what this place looks like. "The *walls* are peeling off."

"Yes," she says fondly. "You can see the original wallpaper. Very ornate, isn't it? Doesn't it make you feel like we've traveled back to the 1890s? We're going to *love* living here."

Evan gives a snort of disbelief.

"Whatever," he says.

a voice
like a hand

shaking me

out of sleep

deep

raw

young

male

Has he come back?

*the front
door*

is

open

the air

           moves

      fresh

           aroused

his voice has pricked

the layers of my peace

now bristles are

popping the seams

of my silence

sawdust

paint

clatters

metallic

shoutings

thuds

thumps

bangs

screeches

buzzes

my walls,

       faded and friendly,

are stripped

       ripped and gutted,

worse than naked.

              I will not look.

my floors, my rooms, my companions, are littered with boxes
weighted with furniture

I am unsettled

           shelves strain under books

      paintings like wounds on my walls

        frames like scars

      rugs smother my floors

           more and more boxes

     opening

spreading their contents like a stain

That voice again.

He is back.

Upstairs—

he will come upstairs

into his

room.

I will wait
for him here
where

floorboards
recall
furniture and footsteps

walls
remember
words and breath

air
retraces
sweat

and

kisses

he belongs here

So do I.

On official moving day the place still seems shabby to Evan, even though repairs have been going on for several months now and the house is supposedly ready. The air smells like paint, but underneath that is the musty odor of old wood, varnish, and neglect. Evan knows they don't have nearly enough furniture to fill the house, and that many rooms will remain empty. He has a sneaking suspicion that Mom's burned most of the divorce settlement getting this heap even halfway livable.

The movers are bringing the last load. Mom, Evan, and Libby come in together. Evan, ever practical, is carrying a box of his own belongings. Mom and Libby, empty-handed, prefer to let the movers do all the work.

Mom is the happiest Evan can remember. She stops in the hallway, hands on Libby's shoulders. "Oh," she says, "I can't believe we're finally here."

She has not been like this in a long time, light and smiling and excited about the future. Evan knows she's living out her lifetime fantasy of owning a big romantic old house. And the move doesn't really affect him much—same school, same friends. Besides, the apartment *was* crowded, with the three of them. So Evan has decided to at least *try* to keep his thoughts to himself.

"Isn't it gorgeous?" Mom asks Evan and Libby.

"It's *big*!" Libby agrees happily.

Mom's hand squeezes Libby's shoulder. "It's *ours*!" she says, the words soft and intense like a prayer. And then she grins. "Forget my bedroom," she says. "I'm going to start on my office!"

Libby heads for the stairs. "I'm going to *explore*."

Evan says nothing. Sometimes he thinks he's the only adult in this family.

Mom notices Evan's silence. She glances at him; his feelings are written all over his face. "You know, Evan," she says with a sudden, detached calm, "if you come into this with a negative attitude, it's going to feel like a negative experience. Can't you try to project some positive feelings here?"

Evan's used to counselor-speak. He's grown up with it. He doesn't want to crush his mother's excitement. But he's not going to pretend he's in love with this place, either.

He answers in his own version of counselor-speak. "Just because I'm not as excited as you are doesn't mean I'm negative. Can't I be neutral?"

"Of course." Mom's answer is automatic. "Feelings are always valid." Normally she would pursue the conversation, try to unearth any of her son's hidden emotions about this move. But her eyes are already traveling around the house again; she's too happy to focus on anything else for long. "Oh, look!" she exclaims. "They've unboarded the windows on the landing! Isn't that the most glorious stained glass you've ever seen? And it's original to the house!"

Evan looks. The three windows, halfway up the stairs, have no pictures in them; they're geometric grids with loops and whorls in reds, oranges, yellows, and browns— nice, and they do let more light in, but nothing to get ecstatic about, as far as he can see. He agrees anyway: "Yeah, it's great." And he starts up the stairs with his box.

his room
        is not right

the walls, which should be
        lush with scrolls and leaves,
        are white
        plain

the windows, which should be
        thick with shutters and drapes,
                        are
                        bare

footsteps

on the landing . . .

up the stairs . . .

at the door . . .

van comes into the room, arms flexed, holding his cardboard box. He bends to put it down, straightens, stops to catch his breath and look around. The room is large enough to seem bare even with his bed and desk in it, as well as the boxes that the movers have already brought up. The walls are plain white, as he requested. The windows are empty, without shutters or curtains; he has not decided what he wants to do with them yet.

He is pleased with the windows, though: two on each of two walls, because this is a corner room. They let in lots of sun. He goes to one of the windows, opens it, and looks out over the backyard, which is fairly small and drops down almost immediately to a steep wooded bank overlooking the river.

Evan leans out farther, letting the breeze cool his face.

his hair is too dark
  too oddly long

Why doesn't he push it out of his eyes?
his shirt fits ill
  no collar
    no buttons
his arms bare past the elbows
his knees, his calves

    so bare

    shameless

the windows
let in clear light

he stands there,
a bright flicker
that
draws me

skin touched by sun
tiny golden hairs
a drop of sweat
brow, lashes
curve of jaw
so solid,
so intense—
muscles and bones
like
roots
binding
him to earth.

his breath stirs the air
pulls at me

in

out

in

again

the back of his neck
is warm
smells like wind and sun

tastes
like
salt

he shivers,

standing

in his warm

square of sunlight

*E*van turns to contemplate the sunny room. *It feels strange and foreign to him; not like home—* not yet.

Well, he thinks, *at least it's big. No, what am I saying, it's bigger than our whole apartment.*

He moves to the boxes piled in the center of the room and begins to unpack. The first box is his "stuff"; his posters, personal belongings. He only has a few posters to put up: a video-game advertisement, a scantily clad Budweiser Girl, a football schedule from his high school. He spreads them out, but the walls are still very bare. He takes out an old framed photo of himself and his father at an amusement park; it's always been a favorite of his, but now he's not sure what to do with it.

He and his father have had less and less contact since Dad left a year and a half ago. At first his father was SuperDad, coming every weekend and a couple of times during the week, taking Evan to ball games and movies and dinner. It took Dad a little longer than it took Evan to figure out that they didn't really have a whole lot to talk about when the movies and ball games were over. And when the awkward pauses started outweighing the fun stuff, Dad just sort of ceased to come around.

It hurts in a way—but it also feels right. That's because of Libby. She was hardly ever included in the father-son outings. Evan knew she was too little, wouldn't have enjoyed it once she got there, would have whined and made everybody miserable—but still, he hated hearing her ask to come along and hearing Dad say no. It wasn't exactly Dad's fault; he had only so much free time, and Evan fit better into his activities. But now it feels more like Libby and Evan are equal, as far as Dad is concerned.

Evan puts the picture aside and pulls out the shoebox in which he keeps things of sentimental value; it contains ticket stubs; notes from girls; a poem he wrote for English that he worked hard on, for once—the teacher read it to the class; a picture of himself and his girlfriend, Carrie, at junior prom; a picture of his grandparents; and a baby toy that he doesn't want anyone to know he kept.

As he's putting this shoebox in a drawer, Libby comes in without knocking. She does that a lot since Mom quit her job, but Evan says nothing; on another day he might be irritated, but today, for some reason, he almost likes the way she wants to be with him, the way she feels at home wherever he is.

Libby walks over to the back windows and leans out, just as Evan did a moment before. "Ooh, you can see all the way down to the river from here."

Evan has decided that he likes this room, or rather, the size of it. He's enjoying filling out his own space however he wants, and he's in a better mood about the house. "Back in the old days, they didn't have air-conditioning," he tells her. "Rich people built their houses up here because it was cooler—see, the breeze comes up from the river."

"Are we rich?"

"I wish." He thinks how much it must be costing to get this hulk fixed up, and figures it's a good thing

Libby likes peanut-butter-and-jelly sandwiches better than steak. "What can you see from your window?" he asks Libby, opening another box.

"The driveway."

"Come on," he says, "you can see more than that."

She's still leaning out the window, taken by the view. "Umm, the house next door."

"That's not a house," Evan informs her. "It's a law office." That's another one of the things Evan doesn't like about this place—it's not a regular neighborhood, but the remnants of one that has been taken over by businesses. "Anyway, you can't complain," he tells Libby. "You had first choice of rooms."

"I like my room," Libby says. "I just wish I could see the river."

Her voice is plaintive. Evan pauses to look at her; she's always been a bouncy, upbeat kid, but ever since Dad left she seems to get sad sometimes. It makes him mad at Dad, although the truth is, he could see why Dad might not be as eager to take Libby to the playground as he was to go with Evan to a hockey game. Evan knows now, from relentless boring experience, that there's nothing fun about sitting around watching a five-year-old swing on a swing set.

Mom hasn't been much better, in Evan's opinion—ever since she quit her job and took Libby out of day care, it looks to Evan like Libby has mostly been left to entertain herself around the house.

Libby never talks about any of this, though, and Evan doesn't know how to ask. That's Mom's department, talking to people about stuff like that.

"You can come look out my window sometimes," he offers.

She turns to look at him, hands still on the windowsill. "Anytime I want?"

"No. You have to ask first."

"I didn't ask just now," she points out, very serious.

Sometimes the way she say things, the way she blinks at him, reminds him of a wise little owl. "That's right, you didn't," he agrees, just as seriously. "You owe me."

"What do I owe you?"

Evan doesn't really want anything. "Um . . . you have to bring me a Coke," he finally says.

"Mom said no food or drinks upstairs," Libby says, obviously quoting, "because we'll spill on the floors, and they're—"

"Don't tell me," Evan says, grimacing. "Original to the house."

quiet
night nestles into corners

tall clock in the downstairs hall
ticks the seconds

I roam.

The floors are dark rivers.
silver and gray
currents
of
moonlight pour
through windows
spill
from one room   to the next.

sofas,

chairs,

boxes,

scattered

like small, battered pieces of shipwreck

the stairs rise
          in
rippling folds

windows on the landing

glow

The door to

his room

is open.

he is in his bed

      not high and soft

but small,

           close to the floor
           hard,
    simple as a sailor's berth

bedclothes

draped and wound

around his limbs

his face smooth in sleep

lips relaxed

boys' lips,

I remember

can be so rough, so tender

so sweet

so soft

so full of lies.

That night, Evan has strange, choppy dreams that come in flashes. He dreams of sex, which wouldn't be unusual except that these dreams have a detailed, familiar feel to them, as if his mind is playing back a memory rather than making up something new.

He also realizes, when he wakes, that he never saw the girl's face. What he mostly remembers is her fine, pale hair. In the beginning it fell in a long braid over her bare shoulder. Later he saw it loose when she was under him and her hands reached up to clutch his arms and shoulders. Unbound, he remembers, it was soft against his nose and lips.

He comes downstairs in the morning to find his mother at the table in the breakfast nook, which is off the kitchen. The dining room itself is large, empty of furniture, and rather dark. Mom has finished eating breakfast and is drinking coffee. She looks relaxed and pleased with life in general. She has the house of her dreams, the job of her dreams, and happily she is unaware that her son has been having dream-sex with a hot young blonde all night.

"Good morning," she says.

"Morning," says Evan.

"Doughnut?"

"No, thanks." He gets some milk out of the refrigerator, and a glass. He pours the milk, then starts drinking it the way he always does, in one long series of gulps.

His mother takes a sip of coffee. "You look tired," she tells him.

"I had a lot of dreams."

"About what?"

"I don't remember." He does remember; he just has no intention of discussing this with her.

It's summer, but Mom keeps both hands wrapped around the cup. She always does that, as if she enjoys the warmth. "You should keep a dream diary," she advises.

"Yeah, I should," Evan agrees, but he doesn't mean it.

Mom sips her coffee again, then sets the cup down with a careful clunk. "I'll pick you up a journal, if you want. I'm about to get out and go sign Libby up for swim lessons."

"About time," Evan says without thinking. Immediately he knows he shouldn't have said it. It occurs to him now that Mom *has* been busy getting the house ready, picking out paint colors, meeting with workmen, signing papers. Now that they're here, of course she'll have more time to do things for Libby.

Mom's hands are still on the cup, but she's intent on him now. "What's that supposed to mean?"

"Nothing," he tells her, but then figures since it's halfway out, he might as well finish. "It's just that you moved her away from all her friends, and there's nobody for her to play with around here. And the Asshole never comes to see her."

Mom grips her cup a little tighter, and the look she gives Evan could nail him to the wall. "Don't call him that," she says in her put-your-foot-down voice. "He's your father." She starts to take another sip of coffee, but stops with the cup halfway in the air. "And you know something? You are not the parent here, Evan."

"Sorry," says Evan. He's not sorry, not really. And he adds to himself, as he walks off, *but he really is an asshole.*

This house

and I

we fret.

everything is odd and wrong

rooms
  that have
    breathed their own

  rhythm

      are now
        stuffed
        smothered

           the back parlor is
     a messy nest
                    of tables, desks, books

        scribbled scraps
     of paper
                 cling together in
          piles

mirrors are
no longer snugly
blanketed with dust
but undraped
reflecting sharp, clear,
jagged movement

mirrors are
no longer snugly
blanketed with dust
but undraped
reflecting sharp, clear,
jagged movement

doors long closed
            are now
    open

air, long solid and settled,
                is
                        tossed and whirled

by
        unpredictable
    breezes

windows, frail and thin,
  are unboarded

afternoon light
  pushes
  through the panes
trickles down
the
 stairs

uneven drips

of

voices

write that down

come here and let me

fix

cartoons

Mama

I got it

just another minute

yes, we do

two for five dollars

put
it back when
you're done

is this blue or purple

Evan! Phone!

his
voice is
husky, rough

it ripples the air,
winds itself
around me
clings
tugs at me

Evan's on the phone with his girlfriend. He's been going out with Carrie for about a year, which is a long time compared to most people they know. She was the first girl he ever had the nerve to ask out, his first date, his first steady, his first sex. They've always been crazy about each other, and back when they first started going out, he couldn't keep his eyes off her. Couldn't keep his *mind* off her—even during finals, he'd be impatient to finish so he could get out into the hall and find her, just to be with her. He liked the intent way she listened, eyes fastened to him; the way she made him feel smart, funny, important, strong. With most girls he felt like he was onstage; all he had to be with Carrie was himself.

Nowadays, Evan has noticed, he talks to Carrie more when they're on the phone than when they're together. Sometimes he says things he didn't realize he was thinking until the very moment he says them aloud. It gives him a vague feeling that he doesn't even *know* what he thinks until he puts it into words and says it to her.

"Yeah, we're pretty much moved in," he's telling her. "No, it's a lot better now. It's not a total pit. Believe me, it was. Mom was all, 'Look at the paneling, it's original to the house.' But it looks okay now. Like human beings live here instead of spiders and bats."

While he's talking, he decides to go downstairs and get something to drink. He's on the cordless, so he won't have to hang up.

As he walks across the room, he gets a chill; sometimes there's a draft in here, but he hasn't figured out yet where it's coming from.

this room
the windows the walls
all wrong somehow
        odd objects everywhere

                and the bed

                        is in the wrong
                    place

oh! the mattress was so soft
the down-filled ticking rose
around us like billowy waves

No!
This bed will have its head
against the wall by the door
the way it always did.

*n the kitchen, Evan leans against the counter, drinking a 7-Up, while Carrie tells him about a fight her parents had. When he's done, he tosses the can and walks back toward the stairs. As he heads up, he sees that Mom's working in her office—or rather, she's staring thoughtfully at the computer screen. That's what she calls working, these days.

When he gets back to his room, he finds that the bed has been moved.

"Hang on a sec." He holds the phone away from his mouth and yells out into the hall: "Will you guys leave my stuff alone!"

With the phone in one hand, he moves the bed back. Sometimes it seems like the women in his life are always in his business. He can't even put his own furniture where he wants.

"I think Mom's gone flaky on us," he tells Carrie

when the bed is back where it belongs. "First she sold her book, then Dad took off, then she quit her job and bought this house. Now she's even beyond all that counselor-sounding shit she used to say. Now she's all about 'Follow your bliss' and 'Jump and the net will appear.'"

As he talks to Carrie, he sees Libby hanging around by the doorway. Next thing he knows, she's all the way in his room, poking around the stuff on his desk.

He covers the mouthpiece—"Hey! Get out of here!"—and then answers Carrie. "Well, the third floor's not fixed yet; the walls are still peeling. Mom's got guys up there working on—Libby, I said get out!"

But Libby's seen a picture on his desk, the one of Evan and their dad at the amusement park. They are together in one bumper car, side by side, Dad's arm slung around Evan's shoulder. They're both grinning happily into the camera. Evan's features are a mirror of Dad's: the same smile takes over his whole face, crinkling up his eyes in the exact same way. The resemblance ends there, though. Dad has the sun-bleached look of an aging surfer, while Evan has Mom's coloring: dark hair, dark eyes.

Solemnly, Libby bends over to peer intently into her

father's face. Libby has Dad's fair hair and blue eyes.

"What?" Evan asks Carrie, but he's watching Libby, who slowly puts out one finger to touch the photo. "Right now? Um, I guess. Let me just shower off real quick, and then I'll be over."

Libby's face is full of longing, and Evan is now feeling bad for snapping at her. "Listen, I've got to go," he tells Carrie. "Yeah, me too. Yeah. Be there in a few."

He shuts off the phone and stands for a moment watching Libby, who seems to have forgotten that he's there. He feels he ought to say something, but doesn't know what; he's not so good with words. He just doesn't like seeing Libby so sad, that's all.

He moves over to his stereo and turns it on. "Hey, Lib," he calls to her. "I got a song you're gonna like. Come here."

Libby looks at him over her shoulder. Evan has always made it very clear that his stereo is off-limits to her. "You're going to let me listen to your CDs?" she asks him, doubtful.

In answer, Evan holds out the headphones. She comes over with tentative steps, unsure what she's done to earn this honor. He gently puts the headphones on her ears. He can't hear the frantic rush of snare and cymbals that signals the beginning of the song, or the thick, shuddering bass that joins in. But he watches as her face loses its sad lines and starts to show that she does indeed like the song. For the moment, he almost doesn't mind that Mom deliberately bought him the edited version of the CD. At least Libby can listen to it.

After a few moments, he lifts one headphone off her ear. "I'm gonna go take a quick shower," he tells her. "Don't touch any buttons. I'll be right back." He places the headphone back, and she stands perfectly still, hands stiff at her sides so as not to touch anything. He moves to get a change of clothes out of his dresser, then goes through the door to the bathroom he and Libby share.

when he moves
      the air behind him
            holds his scent

    I trail along

      delicious

*I*n the bathroom, *Evan locks the door behind him and* turns the water on. He strips his T-shirt over his head, wads it up, and tosses it into the hamper. He already knows that it takes a while for hot water to work its way up here from the basement, so he takes his time getting undressed. He's thinking about Dad, about Libby.

his chest, revealed,
is so smooth
a work of art
unseen
by any other eyes

I remember
my fingertips touched
his shirtfront
the cloth cool, crisp white

undid one
button
my hand slipped in
skin on skin

I remember I
felt his heart
beating
as if it had run
a great distance

oh, I remember

button

after

button

y the time Evan's got his clothes off, *the water still isn't hot*. He stands naked, leaning back against the sink. He's thinking about that little electric car Dad got Libby for her second birthday. Even at fourteen years old, Evan had almost been jealous about how utterly cool it was, a tiny little sports car with a real gas pedal and brake, a real steering wheel that worked. That was so like Dad, to forget things like not letting babies put things in their mouths and then go out and buy something expensive, something unforgettable.

The only problem was that Libby wasn't old enough to drive it. She sat in it and opened and shut the doors and played with the steering wheel and the little horn, but she didn't know to put her foot on the gas pedal. And when Dad reached in and placed her foot on the gas, the car took off suddenly, with Libby unable to steer it, and she'd crashed into the curb. She'd been knocked out of her seat onto the hood, and she'd started crying, scared but not hurt. Dad didn't go to her, didn't say much; he mostly seemed a little angry that his gift hadn't been appreciated. Mom had been the one to pick Libby up and comfort her while Dad ignored Libby and got Evan to help him carry the car back into the house. Then they sat down to watch the game together, and that was it for Libby's birthday.

Finally the water's at least warm, and Evan steps into the shower. He pulls the curtain behind him.

I remember
the warmth of his
skin

when I looked up at him
afraid of my own daring
his eyes were so bare,
intent, needy, hopeful,
that even when
we heard footsteps
outside the door
and burst apart
we were still connected
by this bond
this secret

this beginning

When Evan gets out of the shower, the mirror is steamed up. As he stands in front of it, wrapped in a towel, he sees his own reflection as a vague shape under the gray-white mist on the glass. For a moment it looks like there's something behind him, another vague shape—but when he turns to look, nothing is there. When he wipes the mirror with a hand towel, the only things reflected are himself, the door, and the walls.

After he's dressed in clean clothes, he goes to tell Libby that maybe she can listen to the song again later. He gets his car keys from the dresser, flips the light switch, and heads downstairs.

"Mom," he calls without stopping, "I'm going over to Carrie's, be back by dinner, okay?"

He couldn't get away with that on a school night—she'd be asking him about homework and time frames.

But it's summer, and all Mom says from her computer-staring trance is, "Fine, have a good time."

And so, free, he steps out the front door, letting it bang shut behind him, and leaves the house.

he is

    gone

               gone

    always I am
left behind

    a stone
    in currents that pass

               and flow

                 onward

Carrie's parents are out when Evan gets to her house. Her eyes light up when he comes in. One of the things Evan really likes about her is that she understands that sometimes a guy doesn't have a lot of money to go on dates. She's never minded the times they've had to go to matinees instead of evening movies—and she doesn't even complain when they don't go anywhere at all. Carrie knows that it's all about being together; it's not about flash. She's happy just being in a relationship.

Okay, it's true that once in a while Evan thinks she's more interested in the relationship than she is in him, but then he always tells himself that's just a girl thing, the way they like getting cards and flowers on holidays.

Carrie thinks that her parents will be back in an hour or so, but isn't sure. To Evan, this means they need to have sex right away. As Evan sees it, sex is one of the perks that come with monogamy.

This time it's in Carrie's room, on her bed. Afterward, he rolls over onto his back while she tucks herself up against him, letting one finger play over his chest. These are the times he's always liked best—apart from the sex itself, of course. He likes the quiet ease of it, like floating.

Times like this remind him of last summer, their first summer together. Carrie's mom was out a lot, so he'd come to her house on his days off and they'd make love and then go out back to laze around Carrie's pool all afternoon. Those were some of the best times of Evan's life—exhausting himself trying out new things in his first sexual experiences and then, utterly content, dozing on a floating chaise, aimlessly bobbing, disconnected from everything except the heavy scent of chlorine and Carrie's sunscreen—skin warm, water cool, eyes closed against the bright sun.

It's been different lately, though. This time especially he notices it. Maybe because the sex itself seemed rather flat to Evan, because he can't help but compare it to the dreams he's been having—and he *has* been having them, ever since the move: the same girl, the same bed, the same intense familiarity. With Carrie it feels good, of course, more satisfying than scratching an itch; but when he's done he feels a little uncomfortable, as if he's just used his girlfriend with the same efficiency with which he'd have used his own hand.

He *has* wondered what it would be like to have sex with someone else. But that would mess things up; it would hurt Carrie and she'd get mad and make him feel bad. He doesn't have anybody in mind anyway, just sort of idly wonders sometimes.

He doesn't say any of this, of course. Carrie's watching him. She's been doing that sometimes lately. It's almost as if she's waiting for something. If she is, she never says anything. And Evan never asks.

He puts an arm around her. He doesn't feel like talking to Carrie much in person. On the phone, she is quiet and listens; in person, she seems quiet and needy. He can't put any of this into words, but he feels it, and it makes him inclined to clam up.

He doesn't know how long they've been lying there

before he asks the key question again: "How long did you say it'd be before your parents are supposed to be back?"

"I don't know. Maybe half an hour now?" Carrie answers.

There's a long silence. Carrie is running her finger along his chest. Then she starts circling his nipple with her fingertip.

"What are you thinking about?" she asks.

"I dunno."

Carrie snuggles closer. He's pretty sure his arm is going to sleep, but doesn't want to let on.

"Of course you know what you're thinking about," she tells him. "Tell me."

What is he thinking about? Really?

"My mom," he answers. It's only the truth.

Carrie's finger stops moving. "Your mom? We're lying here, and you're thinking about your mother?"

"Not just Mom," Evan explains. "It's the whole thing. It's the new house. It's Libby."

Carrie's hand is flat on his chest now. She's not looking at his face anymore, but staring at her unmoving hand with a slight frown. Evan takes this as a sign of interest.

"Now that we've moved," he continues, "there's nobody for Libby to play with. At the apartment she could just go next door, or over to the playground. Now there's nobody. It's not even a real neighborhood. There's a law office on one side and an old house that's just open for tours on the other."

It's almost like talking on the phone; he's had all this in the back of his mind, but he didn't know any of it, not really, not until he started saying it aloud to Carrie.

Carrie seems to be considering what he's said. After a moment, she speaks.

"I can't believe," she says, "that you're thinking about this right after we made love."

Evan blinks.

"I mean, here we are sharing this tender moment, and you're thinking about your *mother* and *sister*."

"You *asked*," Evan points out.

Carrie pulls back to look at him. "I know I did." She's got that all-or-nothing look in her eye. "And now

I'm going to be honest, Evan: there's a million kids out there who have to move and who don't live near other kids. She'll be fine."

This is another way it's been different lately. Evan doesn't get to lie there, relaxing contentedly, anymore. Carrie's got to dig up something that she can pick apart. It's not arguing, though—at least that's what Carrie says. It's "discussing."

Evan only wanted to answer her question. But his answer was *wrong*. He should have kept his mouth shut.

So now he doesn't say anything.

Carrie watches him for a second, then nestles close again. "It's nothing against Libby. I'm only saying it because I don't want you to worry. I love you. You know that, right?"

"Uh-huh."

"And . . ." She's watching him again, running her palm slowly back and forth along his skin.

"And what?" He knows what she wants him to say. It feels like a requirement that she's trying to drill into him, like saying *please* or *thank you*.

"And you love me, too?" she asks in a small voice.

"And I love you, too." To Evan, his voice sounds as flat as he feels.

Carrie drops a kiss on his chest. It feels as if she's rewarding him for saying the exact words that she needed him to say.

oh, I am hollow

the house restless
without him

there are others
who won't fade now
they
appear

here

                                        there

        all

                    over the

                house

that one
scuffs around humming
clang, clink
of silverware, porcelain
water
trickling

sun on the sills
    on the white tiles
rich odors

settles into
a wide stuffed chair
                steaming cup in her hands
                stares at
                        notes pinned to the wall
        puts
        her feet up
                releases a sigh
                sips
                eyes blank,
                        turned
                inward

this one
       runs everywhere
skitters chants sings
      never still

                slides
                  down
                    the
                    curve
                  of
                banister

        steps
      the
    up
skips

    up   tiptoe
down   leap

         every
      over   stair in
           the
             house

her hair flies up
like
cottonwood seeds in the wind

when I was little
I ran up and down the stairs
didn't want to wear my hat
hopped outside
poked ants with sticks
chased grasshoppers
ran to hide
among the trees
sneaked away
down the bluff
threw rocks in the river
to see the splash

Mama said I
was running wild
asked Papa to rein me in
he always laughed,
drew me onto his lap
and I kept on
gobbling every moment
like candy
paid no attention
to my mother's worried face
her stream of words
year after year after year:

sit still sit up straight your back should not touch the
back of the chair don't read so much you'll get round
shoulders why don't you work on your embroidery
don't spend so much time outside the wind and sun
will ruin your skin don't run don't bounce don't screech
her voice was ever soft, gentle and low, an excellent
thing in woman

until the day
Mama had a switch cut
from the tree by the cistern
Hold out your hand, she said.
No one had ever struck me.
I ran to Papa but she followed
and said, quiet but firm:

She has no self-control.
And look at her.
She's almost a woman.

My father looked.
He stopped there in the hall
and looked at me, surprised.
He started at the ground,
eyes moving up,
as if seeing me for
the first time:

my shoes, no longer flat, but a ladies' heel
my hemline, hanging almost to the ground
my skirt, bare of pinafore or apron
my waist, nipped and pinched by stays
and there
his gaze faltered.

His face closed.
And he walked away.

her mouth was set, determined
the switch a thin cruel line
that cut the air
whipped my palm

I did not cry.
After that my father was
shy,   removed
awkward, polite
a stranger.

on the stairs
            mid-hop
                        she stops:

little cotton-haired girl
            lonely
            sad

            left behind.

                        No,
                              I
                              don't
                              like
                              these others,
                                    these
                              portraits
                              in flesh
                              and bone

her eyes follow me
lips move
but the words
drift away,
small and fleeting

untethered

When Evan returns from Carrie's, he enters the wide, quiet hall, which is empty except for a potted plant standing in an alcove. He thinks that the broad wooden floors would be a good place for broom hockey, but feels certain that his mother would have a fit if anyone tried it.

As he shuts the door behind him, Libby comes running down the stairs. "Where did she go?"

"Who?" Evan asks.

"The girl."

"What girl?"

"Our company."

Evan looks around. The house is silent, no sound of voices. Down here, he can't even hear the workmen on the third floor. "I don't know," he tells Libby, but then, curious, he walks over to Mom's office to see who is visiting.

Mom sits alone at her computer. For once she isn't staring at the screen, but is typing. She doesn't look up when they come in.

"Hey, Mom—is somebody here?"

Her fingers keep moving. "What do you mean?" she says vaguely.

"Is somebody visiting or something?"

Flustered now, she stops; her fingers hover over the keyboard. "Just the guys working upstairs," she says sharply. "And I thought I saw one of them going out to the truck. He may be back by now, though, I don't know. Why are you asking me this?"

"Because Libby said we have company."

Mom turns to Libby. "We don't have any company, Libby. No one is here."

"But I saw her when I was playing on the stairs," Libby says with certainty. "She was standing outside Evan's room."

Now Mom and Evan are both staring at her.

"You saw someone in the house," Mom repeats, wanting to be sure.

"Uh-huh. It was a girl. She was wearing a white dress."

Mom rolls her chair back and stands up. "One of the workmen must have brought in his daughter or something." She walks through the doorway and out into the hall.

As she heads for the stairs, Libby catches up with her. And after a moment, Evan decides to follow along. He doesn't want to miss a good scene.

"I don't want to be unreasonable," Mom announces to no one in particular as she heads up the stairs, "but we can't have strange kids running around the house unsupervised."

"That's *right*," Libby agrees. She's stomping along eagerly next to Mom.

"Now, you just stay out of it and let me do the talking," Mom warns her. "Understand?"

"Uh-huh."

Evan now feels a little like he's in a circus parade, so he hangs back a bit. By the time he gets to the third-floor rooms, Mom is standing with the only workman up here at the moment, and her hands are on her hips.

But it's her daughter she's looking at. "Libby," she's saying sternly, "I think maybe it was Mr. Estes you saw on the stairs."

"It wasn't a man, it was a girl."

"Hey," says Mr. Estes. "I used to have a pretend friend when I was her age. His name was Rufus," he adds to Libby; apparently Mr. Estes is a genial kind of guy. "What's your friend's name, kid?"

"I don't know. She wouldn't answer me."

"That's okay. Quiet friends are the best kind." He winks at Mom and Evan, and goes back to his work.

Mom turns on Evan. "Evan, did you lock the door behind you when you left?"

"No. What's the point? The workmen are always going in and out."

Mom looks even more displeased. She's about to let loose on Evan, he can tell, when miraculously he is saved by Mr. Estes.

"Oh, by the way, Ms. Calhoun," he says. "We found something behind one of the walls. We weren't sure if you wanted it thrown out or not."

He walks over to a pile of lumber odds and ends and picks up a steel box from the floor. He hands the box to Mom. "We were pulling off plasterboard, and there it was. Looked like there used to be a cabinet, maybe a safe, got boarded up."

"Ooh," Libby says, wide-eyed. "Is it treasure?"

"Nope—sorry, kid," Mr. Estes tells her. "Just a bunch of papers."

"Can I see?" Libby leans over her mother's arm. Mom opens the lid and shows her that it is, indeed, a pile of papers.

"Oh." Libby is disappointed.

Mom's been thinking. "Okay," she says, shutting the lid. "Evan. Just to be safe, will you help me check the rooms? And Libby, I don't even know what to do with you. Do you see how much trouble you're causing?"

"I didn't mean to."

"I know, I know. Just—oh, never mind. Come on, Evan. Mr. Estes, if you hear screams or gunshots, just call the police, please."

That's Mom's weird sense of humor. Sometimes it confuses people, but Mr. Estes just grins and says, "Sure thing."

Of course there is no one in the house. Libby loses interest less than halfway through the search and goes off to her room to play.

Downstairs, the search ends back in Mom's office. "Thank you, Evan," she says, sitting down in her chair again. "Now! If I can just get some work done!" She pulls herself up to her desk, traces of irritation still on her face as she peers at the computer screen, trying to figure out where she was.

Even so, Evan lingers. There's something he feels compelled to point out. "You know, Mom," he says. "Maybe Libby wouldn't be dreaming up fake people if you'd have somebody over for her to play with once in a while."

That gets his mother's attention again. She swivels away from the screen and gives him a look that could curdle milk. "Evan. I work at home now. Just because I'm not punching a clock from nine to five doesn't mean I don't have a job. I'm a writer. I have to write."

"You're also a mother. You could take time to do something for her."

Mom looks stunned. Just for a moment, though. Then her eyes narrow. "So could you," she says coldly. "You're seventeen, and it's summer. You aren't in school and you don't have a job. You have a car—which I bought, by the way, and which I keep insured and full of gas. Instead of judging and complaining, why don't *you* take Libby somewhere to play?"

Now Evan is the one at a loss for words. But only for a few seconds. "Because *I'm* not the parent here!" he snaps at her, and then turns to stomp out of the office.

Upstairs, Evan slams the door to his room and walks around fuming for a bit, unable to concentrate on anything.

It's not fair—he did have a job, last summer. He just hasn't gotten around to having one yet *this* summer— but he will. It's not like he *enjoys* having to ask her for money. It's not like he's had a lot of *time*, anyway, the way she's kept him packing and cleaning.

He just wanted to take a break for a few weeks. God. He made good grades all year. Played two different sports. Worked his butt off. You'd think that would count for something.

Finally he finds himself staring with irritation and guilt at the photo of himself and his dad. It's true: he hasn't done anything for Libby since they've moved. And he should; he's the man of the house now. Instead, he's left Libby to fend for herself. Even more than Mom has, because he has the time.

Dad's there in the photo, smiling. In real life he's gone, off to a hassle-free existence. If he hadn't left, Mom wouldn't be so preoccupied, Evan wouldn't be feeling responsible, and Libby wouldn't be feeling sad. It seems unfair that Evan, Mom, and Libby should be the ones feeling bad and fighting while the one who started it all walked away scot-free.

Evan pulls his keepsake shoebox out of the drawer. He takes the framed photo off the desk and stows it away in the box. As he puts the box back into the drawer, there's a knock at the door.

"What?" he growls.

"Can I come in?" It's Libby.

Evan doesn't really want her to, but he's also feeling

guilty now about never doing anything for her. "All right," he tells her, shutting the drawer.

"Are you busy?" she asks.

"Not really."

"Will you play with me?"

"What do you want to play?"

Libby screws her face up in an expression of futile hope. "Dolls?"

"No," Evan says without hesitation. But Libby is now standing with one hand on the back of the chair, and she's scanning the desktop.

"Where's your picture of Dad?"

"I dunno."

"You didn't lose it, did you?"

"No."

"Well, where is it?"

"In a drawer."

"Why is it in a drawer?"

"Hey," Evan tells her, "dolls it is. Just this once."

Libby's face lights up. "Really?"

Evan sighs. "Yeah. This is it, though. Enjoy it while it lasts."

Libby grabs his hand and tugs him to the door. "Come on! Come on!"

In her room across the hall, she digs through her junk and collects a motley armful of dolls and accessories, which she brings to Evan.

"What do I have to do?" he asks her, not touching anything.

Libby already has a plan. "I'll have Lucinda," she tells him, "and you have Winnebago." She hands him a worse-for-wear doll with long straight hair.

Evan sits on Libby's bed, looking at the doll as if he's never seen one before. "Winnebago?"

"That's her name."

"Why?"

"Because it's pretty. Now." She starts distributing doll clothes. "They're going to go to the ball. Here. Put this on her."

"On Winnebago."

"Right."

Evan sticks the doll's legs into the dress and starts working it up the plastic body. Then he stops. "Promise you'll never tell anybody I did this with you."

"Okay," Libby says offhandedly. She's busy dressing Lucinda.

Evan awkwardly gets the dress on Winnebago and fastened. When he's done, he holds her up for inspection.

"Good!" Libby says with satisfaction. "Now. They're going to go to a party. Lucinda's going to wear *this*." She pulls out another outfit and lays it aside on the bed. "And Winnebago's going to wear *this*." She hands Evan another dress.

"What about the ball?" Evan asks.

"They already went."

"You mean we just sit here and change their clothes over and over?"

Libby's intent on Lucinda's party wear. She doesn't look at him. "We can fix their hair if you want," she offers.

"No. Clothes are fine." Evan starts stripping off Winnebago's ball gown. "Hey, Lib. You know that girl you saw—you know you just imagined her, right?"

"No." Libby says it matter-of-factly, while she's dressing her doll. "I saw her. She was standing in the hall outside your room."

"Maybe she likes the view of the river, huh?"

"I guess." She gives it some more thought. "I don't think she has any friends. She's very lonely."

Evan looks up at that. The doll lies half-dressed in his hand. "What makes you say that? That she's lonely?"

"She looked sad," Libby answers. "Hey, Evan. Can I have that picture of Dad and you?"

Evan looks down at the doll in his hand. He's thinking, *Libby is the one who's lonely; Libby is the one who's sad.* "Why do you want it?" he asks.

"You're not dressing Winnebago," Libby points out, and Evan pulls the doll's dress around its shoulders, then fastens the Velcro. " 'Cause I like to look at it," she tells him.

"Why?"

"I dunno. I just do."

"Let me think about it." Evan holds out a re-dressed Winnebago. "Here we go. Ready for the party."

Libby runs a practiced eye up and down his work. "Okay," she says, satisfied. "Now Lucinda's going to get married. Winnebago can wear this." She hands Evan a doll-sized denim pantsuit.

"She's not a bridesmaid, huh?"

"No, she's in the audience."

"So old Lucinda gets all the glory."

"There's only one bride dress," Libby informs him. She sets to work on Lucinda, which takes a little work because the bridal gown has long sleeves, and although Lucinda's arms are very skinny, her hands are rather large. Evan takes his time with Winnebago. He considers making her moon Libby, but thinks better of it.

"Do you think," Libby asks, "that if Dad had liked me better, he would have taken a picture with me?"

"He did like you, Libby. He still does. He's just . . . busy right now."

"He never comes. Or calls. But he *lived* with us when you were as old as me."

"Hey. Libby. You're not thinking it's your fault Dad left, are you?"

"Uh-huh."

"But it's not. Why would it be? You're just a kid. He's a grown man."

"I haven't figured it out yet." She sounds a little

puzzled. "Maybe I was too noisy. Sometimes I didn't know when he made a joke. I don't know."

"No! Libby, that's stupid. He left because . . . because . . ." Evan wishes Mom was dealing with this, because for all her straight-from-a-book counselor-speak, Mom *does* know how to pin words to things. "Well, because he's an asshole. That's all there is to it."

"You're not supposed to say *asshole*."

"Sorry."

"But I won't tell Mom, because you're playing dolls with me."

"Great. Thanks."

The next morning, on his way to the kitchen, Evan sees that Mom's already in her office. He stops, lingering outside the door. Mom is staring at her computer again. He waits a few moments, but she doesn't see him. "Mom," he finally says, "I'm sorry about yesterday."

Mom turns around. She looks relieved; she's always been big on civility and communication. "Me too," she says quickly. "You've really been a huge help, Evan. I didn't mean to dump adult responsibility on you.

Don't worry, okay?"

"Okay," Evan says. But he's still worried.

"You don't have to take care of Libby. We'll be fine. After I get this manuscript in the mail, I'll work on some play dates for her."

But Evan's been thinking. He takes a deep breath and says, "I'm going to get a job and help out."

"No." Mom's wearing her put-your-foot-down *look*. "We're all right for now, promise. I want you to be free to enjoy your senior year. And Libby—well, I've got to get this book out first." The last words are a little strained, and her gaze darts over to her computer screen.

"Are we low on money?" Evan asks.

"No. No. Not yet."

Evan has noticed that she doesn't seem to be doing much typing lately. Mostly she's been sitting and staring in front of the computer. Now he also notices that the number of gray strands in her dark hair has grown, and that her eyes look tired. "Are you having trouble writing or something?"

Mom doesn't answer for a moment. "It's just that I

want this book to do as well as the first one," she finally says, as frankly as if Evan *is* an adult. "We got lucky that I happened to write something that was picked up for a couple of talk shows. We got lucky that it was on the best-seller list for a few weeks. But now . . . this isn't a hobby anymore, it's my career. It's all on the line—I've dropped everything for this; I've put everything we have, as a family, into it. And I've got to keep producing."

"I think they're hiring night stockers down at the grocery store."

Mom gives him a pained look.

"I'm talking about me, not you."

"Oh. No. We're all right. Promise."

Evan nods, and Mom turns back to her work. He notices the steel box sitting on the shelf next to her desk, among stacks of paper—used and unused—reference books, and boxes of printer supplies. "Have you looked in that box?"

"Yeah." Mom's frowning at the screen, one hand on the mouse.

"Are you going to use it for ideas to write about?"

"No. I'm working on something already, and it's a little deeper than . . ." She rolls her chair over, opens the box, and hands Evan a newspaper clipping.

"'Mr. Robert C. Shannon,'" he reads, "'son of Mr. and Mrs. Shannon of York, Pennsylvania, is visiting Mr. and Mrs. G. J. Royce.' Man, they didn't have much going on in this town, did they?"

"Apparently not." Mom rolls her chair back over to the computer. "You can take that upstairs," she says, with a glance at the box, "and look through it if you want. There's a few old photos. It's an interesting slice of daily life, but I can't use it."

"Didn't you say your new book is about religion or something?"

"The need for religious tolerance."

"Right. Okay. I guess I might take it up, then. Do you need it back?"

"No. Just be careful; the papers are fragile."

Evan carries the box with him to the kitchen, and sets it on the counter while he gets himself the usual glass of milk. After putting the empty glass in the sink, he debates whether to call some friends to see if they're up yet or to go back to his room and hang out until later in the morning.

He ends up taking the box upstairs, where he turns on the radio to hear the last part of his favorite drive-time show. As he listens, he sits at his desk and opens the box. Inside are papers, as his mother said: letters and newspaper clippings. He digs through to find the pictures she mentioned. Both are old-time studio portraits. One, in a brown cardboard cover that opens like a book, is of a family: the father, with a sweeping mustache, seated; the mother standing behind him; the daughter standing at her father's knee. All are looking directly at the camera.

echoes
draw up
   in
   faded wisps

little girl
hair the color
of cotton

woman
hair shining and neat
smooth and slender hand

on the man's shoulder
stiff in a suit
hands on knees

The other picture is a portrait of a fair-haired girl, and the first thing that pops into Evan's mind is the sexual dreams he's been having for the past weeks.

She is perhaps about Evan's age. She could be an older version of the girl with the family—her hair is a little darker, but still obviously blond. She is carefully posed, face in the center of the frame, head tilted delicately at an angle, lips curved in a not-quite-smile. One hand is poised so that the arc of her fingertips seems to just barely brush her chin. She is beautiful.

daytime,
I was
dutiful,

waiting
with bowed head for
my future to lay itself
in my lap,

sitting
careful and subdued
face under hat brim
hands under gloves
heart under linen and silk
while sun and clouds passed me by,

draping
my manners like a curtain between
myself
and
the world.

alone at night,
my mind composed its own
vine-twined towers
rose-grown balconies
romantic, daring rescues

Evan lays the photos aside and pulls the box closer. On top is the newspaper clipping his mother showed him. The date at the top is May 2, 1897:

> Mr. Robert C. Shannon, son of Mr. and
> Mrs. Shannon of York, Pennsylvania, is
> visiting Mr. and Mrs. G. J. Royce.

It sounds impressive, Evan thinks. Like the president or something. You'd think the guy was a CEO, or a bigwig back East, and that's why it was in the paper—except that the clipping seems to be a whole column of who's visiting who. There really *wasn't* much going on back then.

I remember he was
so beautiful,
strong and lively
he woke the settled air
stirred the muffled bindings
of the house

*H*e sets the clipping down and picks up one of the letters. It's written by a woman and fairly dull, except for a bit toward the end:

> . . . *I feel certain that if only Robert can stay with you for a few months, away from bad influences while his father calms down, then all will be well and we can reasonably discuss what to do about school in the fall. Robert is not bad, just high-spirited and impulsive.*

Ooh, little Robbie Shannon's been a naughty boy! thinks Evan. *Sounds like the guy got expelled.* But the rest of the letter gives no clue:

Your darling girl has blossomed so in the past year or two; if only Robert had a chance to do the same. I have been heartened to hear how your guidance has enabled Cora to set aside her childish disposition and take up womanly tasks and ways. What a good example she would be for my Robert! The presence of a virtuous female always has a naturally gentling effect on boys; I can certainly attest that Robert never gets into any trouble here at home when he is under my influence.

I am certain that Robert would not be the only one to benefit from this plan. Cora would find in my son the protector and guardian she would have had, had she a brother.

I know I can be frank with you. Mr. Shannon feels strongly that Robert should go to live with his grandfather. Mr. Shannon has always believed that sparing the rod spoils the child, but Robert's grand-

father is of an even sterner generation, and I
fear his use of some of the crueler methods of
discipline that were in use during his own
childhood. . . .

Evan wonders what "crueler methods" might be. He wonders if Cora was the hot chick in the picture, and almost feels a twinge of . . . something.

Possessiveness?

Ridiculous.

He shuffles through more of the letters, looking for clues, but finds none. In fact, most of the letters are not very interesting; they contain mostly daily trivia and religious platitudes couched in heavy Victorian language.

He leafs through a few more; then, bored, decides to go grab a snack and see if Mom's off the computer so he can get online. He leaves the papers scattered on his desk.

I remember
his face was young
but his eyes were
wise

when we sat, prim,
I couldn't help
sneaking a glance at him.
He saw me,
smiled, said nothing,
and didn't seem
to mind.

The days passed and
when he spoke, the sound of
his voice brushed over me,
soft and teasing
filling the stifled, leaden room
with a lightness that couldn't be touched.

When he listened, intent,
leaning forward,
his eyes charmed and coaxed
my words out of their constraints.

When he smiled,
it was a flash that spun
and drove its way
into my chest,
caught my breath,
whirled it up
then let it go.

There were quiet moments
when he forgot to smile
his eyes were the surface
of a dark sorrow
in which he flailed alone,
thinking no one saw.

But I did.

If I forgot and my words
tumbled out,
neither veiled nor polished,
bearing their meanings
like homespun cloth upon their backs,
he laughed, unshocked.

Before he came I
was small and stifled,
tightly hobbled,
but something in the way he laughed
made cords loosen
and fall away.

he didn't steal a kiss
but gave one
just
a touch
a soft lingering
a mere turn of a key
in the lock

and I, who had been
cramped
as if in a cage
a sedate, careful, measured
cage
began to burst out in
secret, joyful ways

doesn't
            love
mean
            trust
            faith
            giving of yourself?

doesn't love mean
            filling a gap
            meeting a need
            completing the whole?

*E*van gets busy with other things, and doesn't come back upstairs till almost bedtime.

When he enters his room, he finds the contents of the metal box neatly inside, the lid shut. He thought he'd left them out on his desk, but doesn't really remember. He thinks about looking at the portrait of the girl again, but doesn't. It's a little creepy, the way he feels drawn to it—that old picture of someone long dead.

Late in the night he falls into a restless doze. He dreams of the girl again, but the flashes are more vivid: the feel of thin, delicate white cloth crumpling in his hands as he shoves her nightgown above her waist; the hot smell of lavender rising up from the sheets; her muffled, rhythmic gasps next to his ear.

They're so intense that he rouses almost to wakefulness, but not quite. Enough to know it's not real, and to be frustrated. Not enough to touch himself, to finish the job.

When a deeper sleep finally overtakes him, he dreams he's lying there and she's nestled next to him, tucked into the curve of his arm, one finger tracing designs on his bare chest. It's quiet, familiar, even though the hair spilling over his arm isn't brown like Carrie's, it's pale and fine and long, still partly in a braid, a mussed-up braid that's come almost undone.

moonlight washes him in silver
arm flung wide in sleep
careless
his breath draws soft and deep
slow, untroubled sighs

*A*nd then, in the dream, in the quiet, he hears something; he's alert with fear, listening: someone is coming and he's about to be caught, caught with this girl and he's perfectly, utterly still, straining to listen into the silence.

I like it when
            his breath
becomes

                        uneven
    like a sob

when he grows cold
            pulls the covers
up to his neck

*I*n the morning, Evan wakes to a slight uneasiness, a sense of dread that doesn't fade when he opens his eyes. He can't remember why he feels this way. All he remembers is the sex.

He rolls over to sit up on the edge of the bed. The box is exactly where he left it last night. The lid is still shut. He doesn't know why he can't shake the feeling that the girl in the box—the girl he's never seen before—is the one in his dreams.

What a creepy idea, considering she probably got old and wrinkled and spotty and became somebody's grandma. And there's no reason to think that the girl in the letter is the one in the picture. And why does he think she's hot anyway, in that dress with the collar up to her chin?

It's sick, that's what it is.

✗ ✗ ✗

It's a few days later when Carrie comes to see the house for the first time. Evan has not invited her before because, quite simply, it did not occur to him. He would not have thought to do it now, a month after moving in, if she had not asked.

When the doorbell rings after dinner, Libby, excited to have company, appears at Evan's side.

He ignores her—Libby is one reason it never occurs to him to have Carrie over; Mom is another—and opens the door.

Sometimes, like today, it hits Evan all at once how lucky he is to have Carrie. She's totally hot, with a great body; Evan is the only one who knows *exactly* how great it is. Her makeup is subtle and perfect. Her brown hair is freshly brushed and shining. Any guy would be lucky to have her.

But not just any guy does. *He* does.

"Hi," he says to her. "Come on in."

Carrie comes in and cranes her neck, looking all around at the airy hall, the ornate stairs leading to the landing. The stained glass makes it look like an altar.

"Wow," she says, impressed.

"Your hair looks like Winnebago's," Libby tells her solemnly.

"Winnebagos," Carrie repeats. Evan can't tell what she's thinking. Sometimes Carrie is easily hurt; sometimes she takes things in stride.

"It's supposed to be a compliment," he informs her. "Just take my word for it."

"Okay." Today must be a taking-in-stride day, because Carrie turns to Libby and gives her a smile. "Thanks, I guess."

Evan is relieved. "Are you ready for the tour?" he asks.

"Yes."

Libby bounces along behind as Evan leads Carrie through the downstairs. "This used to be a parlor," he says, showing her an empty room off the hall. "Mom says someday she's going to get a piano and put it in there."

They move from room to room: the TV room, the dining room, the kitchen. Outside his mother's office, he whispers to Carrie, "Don't ask her when she's going to finish unpacking, because she already has." Then he steps into the open doorway. "Hi, Mom," he says. "Carrie's here."

Mom actually turns away from her computer. "Hi, Carrie. How have you been?"

"Fine, Ms. Calhoun."

"Come on," Evan tells Carrie, "I'll show you the upstairs." He's already moving away.

"Remember the rule," Mom warns him.

"I know."

As they head for the stairs, Carrie asks, "Which rule is that?"

"The 'doors are to remain open at all times' one. Mom thinks that will keep us from"—he glances at Libby, who is running to catch up—"doing certain things."

"Well, it'll keep me from doing certain things, that's for sure. I could just see your mom or sister walking in on us."

"It *could* depend how fast we were, though, couldn't it?"

"No, I'm serious. Don't even think about it. I really do want to see the house, anyway."

"Don't even think about what?" Libby asks, tailing them up the stairs.

Evan sighs. He can't ask Libby to leave them alone,

because Mom relies on Libby, as well as the open-door rule, to be a deterrent to premarital sex.

She's a good one, too. "Carrie! Carrie! See my room?" Libby darts ahead, leading the way. "Want to see my pictures? Look, I drew this one of a butterfly. He's eating the flowers, see?"

"Oh, yes. It's very colorful," Carrie assures her.

"And here he's pooping them out. That's colorful too, isn't it?"

"Yes," says Carrie weakly. "Colorful."

Evan groans. "God, Libby!"

"Oh." It dawns on Libby. "I'm sorry. I'm not supposed to talk about poop to company," she explains to Carrie.

"Hey, Lib," Evan says quickly. "Why don't you dress Lucinda up in that bride dress so you can show Carrie?"

"Oh! Okay!"

Mercifully, she starts digging in her doll bin. Evan knows it will take her a few minutes at least to get that dress on. He pulls Carrie across the landing. "This is my room," he says, walking in. He's actually made the bed for once, in honor of company. The bedspread is folded back over white sheets; the pillow is white, lying neatly on top. For a second he flashes on his dreams, the closest thing to sex he's ever had in this room, and for one knee-trembling second he allows himself to think of ripping the covers back and flinging Carrie onto the bed, onto those white sheets.

Of course he can't. Still, he keeps Carrie's hand in his.

She turns her head, looking around the room. "Um. It's very—what's the word?"

"Homey?"

"Spartan."

"Is that bad?"

Her gaze falls on the Budweiser Girl. "I really don't care for your choice of artwork."

Evan doesn't want to get into a "discussion." He gives her hand a little squeeze. "It's okay. It reminds me of you."

"Me with about twenty pounds of silicone, you mean."

Evan glances over to the door. They're alone. He steps closer to Carrie, close enough to feel her hair against his nose and lips. It's dark and it's not fine, it's wavy and thick, but he says, very low, "No, just you." If nothing else, he's going to get at least a kiss before Libby comes back.

his whisper touches her
                    ear

his breath warm
his lips
all tender curves

his fingers are

entwined with hers

skin against skin

I remember
among the trees
along the bluffs

under the trees,
giggling
turned to
kisses
turned to
touching
turned to
caught breath

over
his shoulder
I watched
the leaves above us
grasping
pieces
of sun,
tossing them,
letting them go

on
his shoulder
my fingers
clutched
white cloth
straining, then
letting
it

go

after that,
whenever I looked
his eyes were on me
full of purpose
and a question
to which I was
the only answer

I remember
easing silent into his room
as if slipping a leash
muted straining passion and then
slick and salty
sweat cooling on his chest
along his neck
while we whispered
always careful
always quiet
tenderness unlocked
and shared.
In the dark he spilled
raw, half-formed thoughts
and words which, always
being held back,
had rusted for lack of use.

I remember
tiptoeing, soundless
before dawn,
past my parents' closed door
my father's even snores
my mother's undisturbed silence.
Back in my own room
I was
still wrapped in closeness
and in kisses.

his lips
on
her lips

just a touch
a soft
lingering

the air
feels wild and thick

I am being slowly squeezed

I remember . . .
what?

a voice knotted in panic

a hand,
hard and harsh
unyielding
weight

arrie pulls back suddenly, looking at the open door.

"What's wrong?" Evan asks.

"Libby," she whispers.

Evan walks quickly to the doorway. He steps outside. No one is there.

He looks across the landing to see Libby in her room, still struggling with Lucinda's dress. "I don't think it was Libby," he tells Carrie, coming back in.

"I thought—I thought I saw somebody. I saw—I don't know."

"Was it purple?"

"I don't know. It was too quick. I just saw it out of the corner of my eye."

"Libby's wearing that crappy old purple T-shirt that was mine about a billion years ago. God, I hate that thing."

"Maybe it was—maybe I imagined it."

"Sometimes, when a car drives by, light gets reflected in weird ways through that stained glass."

"Okay. Well. Do I get to see the rest of the house?"

"Sure."

Evan takes her hand again. As they walk across the room, Carrie says, "Hey, what's that?"

"Old letters and stuff. It was in the attic," Evan tells her without looking around. Only then does he glance over his shoulder at the slightly rusted metal box on his desk. "You mean that box, right?"

"Uh-huh."

"I think it belonged to the lady that used to live here," he adds, as they walk out the door.

Carries follows him onto the landing. "The one that went into a nursing home?"

"No, the one before that."

"Lots of old ladies."

"No, there's only been two owners. And then nobody lived here for a long time."

Evan shows her the other bedrooms, and the unfinished third floor. Libby joins them, eliciting satisfying oohs and aahs from Carrie over Lucinda's gown. They all end up downstairs, watching a movie, with Libby popping in and out just often enough to keep Evan from trying anything. Finally, when it's almost Carrie's curfew, Evan walks her to her car. He kisses her good-bye.

When he stops, she keeps her arms fastened around his neck. "I love you," she says into his ear.

"Me too." His hands are on her waist.

"I don't know what I'd do without you," she says, still clinging.

"Me neither," he agrees, looking into her eyes—but what he's thinking is that he never finished going through that box with the pictures. Finally she lets go and gets into her car. He waves as she backs out; then he walks into the house.

Now that Carrie's safely off, Evan goes up to his room. The metal box is still there, the lid still shut. He hasn't looked at her in several days, and now the thought of her draws him.

He puts on a CD, and then sits at the desk and opens the box. A newspaper clipping now lies on top:

Miss Cora Royce Dead

Miss Cora Royce, aged 16, died in her sleep on Friday past. The remains were embalmed by Embalmer Krentz of this city and will be interred at Roseland Cemetery.

Miss Cora was the daughter of Mr. and Mrs. G. J. Royce and was endowed with all the graceful and amiable traits of young womanhood; she was sweet and gentle in her demeanor and was universally admired and loved by her acquaintances.

he fumbled his hand
over my mouth

his body heavy
like stone

hand crushing

frantic

harder

his face above me
broke into tiny

pieces of light

*T*he obituary gives Evan a cold chill. *He thinks,
If that's her, she died not long after that
picture was taken.*

Evan remembers the name Royce from some of the
other papers; now he shuffles through the pages, picking up letters and skimming through them, skipping
parts that look uninteresting, looking for anything
about this girl who died so young.

He rereads the bits about the visitor from Pennsylvania. Then, under the blare of the music, he scans
more letters, looking for pieces that will pull the story
together. He finds two passages that seem to mention a
sudden death:

> . . . *Words cannot express how sorry we are
> for your loss. We fear that Robert may be a
> burden to you at this time, and so ask that he*

return to us. We have been so grateful for
your hospitality . . .

. . . Robert has matured since the events of
the summer. He does not say much, but I
know he grieves the loss of his new friend. I
wish your darling could know how wondrous,
how beneficial were the effects of her short life
on others, and I hope that your knowing of it
will be a comfort to you in these times . . .

No other letters appear to touch on the subject. He digs through to find the photo of the girl. He finds himself inspecting her face. Her lips especially draw his attention: they are not quite smiling, full, and maybe, he thinks, even slightly parted. The more he looks at them, the more real her face seems, and after a while he finds himself trying to evaluate the lines of her body under her stiff white dress, trying to line them up with what he remembers of his dreams. He bends over the picture, so engrossed that it takes him a few moments to realize what a perv he is, getting hot over a dead girl.

Evan sets the photo down again. He decides, with no evidence, that Robert and Cora must have been *doing it*.

In Evan's dreams that night, everything is clearer. He can see the room around him—it's his room, only different, the walls dark with designs, the windows heavy with curtains and shutters. The bed is different, too—bigger, anchored by a heavy footboard and even heavier headboard. But the sheets are still white.

And the girl has a face. It's the one in the photo. His hands are in her hair. He pulls her under him for slow kisses, but she impatiently fumbles up her nightgown. Her legs are eager, wrapping around his, urging him on.

in the night
           his breath
                    explodes in
                            ragged
                                    bursts

I like the way
           his hands clench
                      the sheets

I like to watch
           his hips jerk
                    straining
                          at nothing

*A*fterward, in his dream, they're lying together, her fingers tracing patterns on his bare chest.

And then she's angry, hitting him, and he grabs her arm, he thinks he hears something outside, but she won't be quiet, she's still trying to hurt him, so he has to put his hand over her mouth to listen.

The creak of a footstep on the stairs. He goes rigid with silence, but she's trying to bite his hand, struggling, so he presses harder, letting his weight muffle her movements to small flutters, and he puts his lips by her ear, wanting to shush her but he doesn't dare speak, so he just lies unmoving, waiting in dread to see if someone is coming.

my chest
hot
bursting

it hurt

I like to hear

his

heart

tick

in

his

chest

like

a

clock
wound
tootight

*I*n the morning, Evan wakes up bleary-eyed. *He clearly remembers the now-usual sex dreams,* but of the rest, all that has stayed with him is the feeling of nightmare, of a struggle to control, to contain, to keep something bottled up and hidden.

It's disturbing, the way feelings are starting to spill out of the dreams and over into waking moments—as if there's a pattern already in place and, through dreams, it's slowly wearing a groove into his mind.

When he sits up and moves to the edge of the bed, he sees that during the night, a few pieces of paper have fallen from his desk onto the floor. He picks them up. They're actually one piece of paper, a page of one of the letters, that somehow in its fall has come apart along the brittle folds.

It's the page about the beneficial effect of the darling daughter's death on Robert.

That's cold, Evan thinks. *Just plain cold. Like her death has meaning only because of this guy's reaction to it.*

This time when he puts the pieces back in the box, he decides he's not going to look at *any* of this anymore. It makes him uncomfortable, uneasy. It gives him nightmares, gives him weird ideas. It disturbs his sleep.

He carefully picks up all the letters and clippings, and sets them back into the box. He hesitates for a moment, his fingers on the cold metal of the lid, then shuts it and pushes the box aside. Evan is now determined: he's not going to think about the girl again.

Over the next few weeks he still has the dreams, but he tries to shove them down as soon as he wakes up. He's busy with other things anyway, *real* things: meeting friends for pickup games of football, for hockey in the school parking lot, for all-night video-game parties. He takes Libby to a movie once, sees Carrie a few times, runs a couple of errands for Mom.

freely he comes

freely goes

freely breathes

lives

freely

why is it

that he

goes on

to breathe

touch

love?

if only I could have

one more breath

one more exhale

one more word:

Unfair.

Evan finds himself forgetting to call Carrie. It crosses his mind, but always when he's already busy doing other stuff.

And then when he *does* remember to call her, instead of being glad to hear from him, she's mad at him for not calling sooner. He's starting to feel like she's always looking at the ways in which he comes up short as a boyfriend. Like he's an imperfect specimen that's got to be whacked and prodded into shape.

It makes him not want to call her at all.

But he does love her, of course he does. She's his girlfriend, isn't she? She's always there in the back of his mind—it's just that they've been together so long, she's so much a fact of his life, that he knows he can count on her always being there. *That's* why he doesn't actively think about her much. It's completely normal.

Isn't it?

"*Evan,*" *Mom says,* "*I need to go run a couple of errands.* Will you watch Libby, please?"

Evan frowns. "I was thinking about going over to Carrie's." He *was* thinking about it, for once. He has not had sex in a week and a half. He *needs* to see her.

"Can't you go after I get back? I'll be back within two hours, promise."

"Can Carrie come over here?" Now that he thinks about it, he likes the idea of being able to do it in his room. On *his* bed.

Just like in the dreams.

"While I'm gone? You know that makes me uncomfortable."

"Libby's going to be here. You know she'll stick to us like caffeine to coffee."

"Can't it wait until I'm back?"

"What do you think, we're going to have wild sex all over the house with my little sister hanging around? Give me some credit, Mom."

Mom says nothing, clearly wavering.

"If you're so worried about it, you can ask when you

get back. You can walk in and say, 'Hey, Carrie, did you have wild sex with my son while I was gone?'"

"All right, all right. I trust you."

"I'm not going to do anything I wouldn't do if you were here," Evan says. *Except have wild sex all over the house*, he thinks as she walks out of the room.

So he calls Carrie up. She sounds glad to hear his voice—no complaints about how he should have called before now—and agrees to come over. All is set, except for one small thing.

He stands at the door of Libby's room. "Hey, Lib. Listen, Carrie's about to come over. Do you think you could leave us alone and not bug us?"

Libby has all her stuffed animals lined up on the bed. She stands in front of them with a notepad and pencil. "I dunno." She makes some marks on the pad.

"Please?"

Libby tears the top paper off and places the page in front of the elephant. Then she turns to Evan. "I will if you play dolls with me again."

"Okay."

"Today?"

"Tomorrow."

"All right. I'll leave you alone." Libby starts scribbling on her pad again.

Satisfied, Evan goes downstairs to hang out in the TV room and wait. When the doorbell rings, he goes to answer it—and here comes Libby, pounding down the stairs to see who's coming to visit. "You're going to play in your room while Carrie's here, right?" he reminds her, heading for the door.

She slows, hesitating on the bottom step. "I guess."

"You guess?" He stops, hand on the doorknob. "Come on, Libby. You said you'd leave us alone, remember? And I said I'd play with you tomorrow?"

"Ye-es," Libby says slowly. "Do you promise?"

"Promise."

"Cross your heart?"

"And hope to die," Evan says, crossing his heart solemnly.

Libby turns to plod back up the stairs, and Evan opens the door. "Hi," he says to Carrie. She looks terrific. She's smiling. She's wearing the necklace that he bought her for Christmas last year, the one he blew the last of his savings on. Now that she's here, he's glad she came. "Want anything to drink?" he asks.

"You got anything diet?"

"Yeah, I think so. Let me go check."

Carrie waits in the hall. When he comes back through the swinging door, she's wandered over to the stairs and is looking at one of the carved balusters that ends in a great swirl on the floor.

He hands her a can from the refrigerator. "See that spindle that's turned upside down? Mom said the guys who made the woodwork did that on purpose, as a sort of signature."

"Huh. I didn't even notice. That's interesting."

Evan watches her pop the top, take a sip. Her lips are full, pink, faintly glossy. "You're beautiful, you know that?"

She lowers the can, smiles. "If you keep saying stuff like that, maybe I won't be mad at you anymore."

"Are you mad at me?"

"Well, I haven't heard from you in a week."

"I haven't heard from you, either. Are you saying the guy has to be the one who calls all the time?"

"No . . ."

"Okay, then. Come on, let's go upstairs."

"Is your mom home?"

"Nope."

"Libby?"

"Yup. I'm in my official capacity as babysitter." Evan leads the way up to his room. They pass Libby, playing in her room with the door open. Evan peers at her as he shuts the door to *his* room.

"I see you've still got that box of letters," Carrie says.

"Yeah."

"Did you ever look through it?"

"Yeah. Most of that stuff is crap, but some of it is like a mystery. See, the lady who it all belonged to, she had a daughter. And this guy came to visit—see, his mom sent him because he was getting wild, like getting expelled from school. And I think when he got here, he and the daughter started getting it on, and then she died, and he was so freaked that he kind of settled down."

"What makes you think they were getting it on?"

Evan flashes back to his dreams. "I dunno."

"People didn't have sex outside of marriage back then, Evan."

"How do you know?"

"They just didn't."

She says it with certainty. Carrie's better in school than he is, and knows more about history and stuff like that. He doesn't like the way she said it, though, like he should have known that already.

He also doesn't want to get into an argument—a *discussion*—right now. "Okay. How about this? They were in love, and it broke his heart when she died, so he took a vow of celibacy and then followed her to the grave."

"Much better."

The knob turns with a click, and the door swings open. It's Libby. Evan is glad he's nowhere near Carrie. Still, she zeroes in on Carrie's Diet Coke can. "You're not supposed to have drinks up here," she informs Evan.

"Carrie's company."

"You're supposed to leave doors open when she comes over."

"Okay, it's open," he says evenly. "You can go now."

But Libby plunks herself down cross-legged outside the open door.

"Libby." Evan's getting irritated. "You promised you'd leave us alone."

"I am leaving you alone. I just want to play right here."

Evan goes out into the hall and pulls Libby out of sight of the doorway. "Listen," he tells her. "If you go downstairs and watch a movie all the way to the end, I'll give you something."

"What?"

"What do you want?"

"A dollar."

Evan thinks about it. "I'll give you *five* dollars if you watch a whole movie *and* if you don't tell Mom."

"You want me to tell Mom a lie?"

"No, no. I just don't want you to bring it up."

"But what if she asks?"

"She won't."

"But what if she does?"

"If she asks you whether Carrie and I were alone together with the door shut, you can tell her yes. You don't have to lie."

"Will I still get the five dollars?"

"Yes. But only if *she's* the one who brings it up. If *you* bring it up, you get nothing. And I won't ever play dolls with you again. Got it?"

"I guess so."

"Okay. I'll walk downstairs with you and help you put on a DVD. What do you want to watch?"

"Um. *Lion King*."

"Be right back," he calls to Carrie. And a few minutes later, when he walks in, she's sitting on the edge of his bed, looking at his football poster. "We have maybe an hour," he tells her, pulling the door shut behind him. "But we'll have to be quiet, because I guarantee it won't take much to get her back up here."

"Maybe we shouldn't."

"Maybe we *should*."

"Maybe you ought to say it again."

"Say what again?"

"What you said downstairs."

Evan sits down beside her and leans over to nuzzle her neck. "You're beautiful."

a mere turn of a key

in

the

lock

e pulls back to look at Carrie. Evan knows in the back of his mind that it really isn't wise to start now, not with Libby in the house.

But this moment—or something very like it—has been dangled in front of him many nights.

Carrie tilts her head and leans in for a kiss.

He gives in. He really wants this; it's all set, it's just too good to pass up. The pattern has already been imprinted here: it feels as if it's in the room, in the walls, the floorboards, the very air—it's ready for him, and all he has to do is let his body follow and fill it in.

I remember
he pulled his shirt
    off

               pulls his shirt
                    off over his head
               one eager movement

white sheets

               white sheets
               crumple tangle

he kicked them off

               kicks
                    them off
               impatient

I remember
my arms locked
around

                    arms lock around
               his neck

gripping

gasping

          plunges

sweat

slicked

        skin

The pillows are getting in the way so without stopping Evan shoves them onto the floor, and one knocks the metal box off the desk with a loud clatter, and he knows he should stop and check for Libby, curious, nosy Libby, or at least wait and listen to see if she's coming, but he doesn't want to, doesn't want to stop, can't stop, he *can't* stop, so he buries his face in Carrie's hair, her neck, and continues till it's finished.

The moment spent

lazy, intertwined
in the quiet,
the gap filled,
the need met,
the whole . . .
not quite
complete

one
small
important
missing
piece . . .

*E*van knows he ought to get up and get dressed, because the door has no lock. But he's lying there relaxed, floating, after some of the best sex he's ever had. He pulls the sheet up to cover them and puts his arm around Carrie.

It takes him a moment to notice that she is not acting like she usually does. She's curled up against him— but she's completely still, completely silent.

"Anything wrong?" he asks.

Carrie does not answer. The best sex Evan has ever had doesn't seem to have made much of an impression on her. She looks like something's bothering her.

"What is it?" Evan asks. "Did I hurt you?"

"No."

"Well, what's wrong?"

"I don't know. It's just that I haven't seen you in a while, and, well . . . have you ever noticed that every time we see each other, we end up having sex?"

Evan's insides start to sink. Of course he's not going to be allowed to stay in that floating daze. No, Carrie's got to pick the moment apart, find something wrong, suck all the perfection out of it. "And that's bad?" he asks.

"No . . ." But she draws the word out, leaving it hanging in the air.

"So what are you saying?" Evan says abruptly. "That you don't want to have sex anymore?"

"No. I guess I'm just starting to wonder if that's the only reason we're together. I mean, we haven't seen each other in over a week and it's the first thing you want to do. It's why you asked me to come over here today, isn't it?"

"I asked you over because I wanted to be with you."

"But not till your mom was going to be gone."

Evan heaves a great, loud sigh. He doesn't know what to say, or how to fix it. All he knows is, he used to feel good about himself when he was around her, and he doesn't anymore.

She always nags and clings now, turning all the good

stuff sour. And he always has to find the right moment to ease away, a moment that doesn't look too obviously as if he's trying to escape all the sourness.

But this time he's stuck. This isn't Carrie's house. He can't back out quietly, can't wait for an opportunity to get up and leave. He's trapped—this is his home and his room, and he has to stay until *she* gets up and leaves.

"And you never say you love me," Carrie complains, "unless I say it first."

That's his cue, Evan knows. He's supposed to say he loves her again. *I love you*, that's what he's supposed to say.

He's just tired of being pushed to say it.

"See? Even right now, I have to pull it out of you. You never say it on your own."

Evan stares up at the ceiling. He's thinking to himself, *Just let it go. This once, will you drop it and let it go?*

"So. I'm almost afraid to ask. Do you love me, Evan?"

lying together
sweat cooling on his chest
no whispers
quiet and still

        Is anything wrong?

No. I was just
thinking we ought to
be married soon, so I
can go back to Pennsylvania with you
in the fall.

        one arm behind his head
        We can't get married
        I'm only seventeen

But we love each
other

don't we?

he said
nothing

But I love you.
Don't you love me?

*E*van digs his heels in. *He is not going to ease away or change the subject.* And he's not going to say it, either; just this once he's not going to go along quietly and try to fit into Carrie's mold. "Why does everything always have to be about love?" he asks, impatient. "Why can't it ever just be about . . . about being together and enjoying each other's company and having a good time?"

Carrie's shocked into silence. Of course. He's always broken down and said what she needs to hear. Always.

Just not today. He feels like she's attached to him, glued to his side, and it's all pressing in on him.

"Is that all I am to you?" she asks in disbelief. "A good time?"

"God," Evan says, staring at the ceiling. "Sometimes it's not even that."

"What do you mean?"

"That's all you ever say: 'Do you love me Evan, do you love me Evan, do you love me Evan?'"

There's that shocked silence again. And then he can't believe it.

She asks him *again*.

"Well? Do you?"

It all goes through his mind in a flash: how she used to be happy just being with him. How he used to look forward to seeing her, not dread it. How she always finds fault with him now, as if he's not trying hard enough.

Now he's just tired. Tired of the whole conversation, of the whole thing. "I don't know anymore," he tells her, not bothering to pretty it up.

"I never would have slept with you if I'd thought you didn't love me."

Her voice trembles. But there's no sympathy left in him; she drained the last bit of sympathy out of him when she asked it one too many times.

"And I never would have thought I loved you," he informs her, "if you hadn't made it part of having sex."

It's funny, this is one of those times that he doesn't know what he feels until he says it out loud.

"Have you *ever* loved me?" Carrie's on the verge of tears—Carrie, who never cries.

It stings Evan, makes him feel guilty. "How am I supposed to know? If you want somebody and you care about them and you like being around them and you're *used* to being around them, how are you supposed to know if it's love?"

Carrie's face is pale. "It's a simple question. Did you ever love me?"

"You're always saying it's love, so I thought it had to be."

She sucks in a deep, shaky breath. When she exhales, she's able to look at him steadily. "One more time, Evan," she says. "Did you ever love me?"

his answer:
one embarrassed
laugh as if
his heart had
snapped shut

and I knew it had
never been open

van rolls onto his side and props himself up on one elbow so he can look directly at Carrie. It occurs to him in a flash: Carrie *says* she loves him, but she doesn't *act* like she does. Not anymore.

She acts like she's going to make him be the answer to her fill-in-the-blank question.

He didn't really understand till this moment that he's been needing space, and he certainly didn't know why. He didn't realize that one or both of them had changed, or grown, or *something*.

"No," he tells her. "I don't think I ever did."

Carrie's face goes white. Weakly, she tries to slap his face, but he catches her hand, stopping it without any effort, and when she tries to pull it loose, he tightens his grip.

"You *asshole!*" Her voice rises into a screech.

Evan remembers Libby, who wouldn't stay in her

room, and he realizes that he's naked, the sheets mostly on the floor, and that there's no lock on the door. "Will you be quiet!" he hisses; he thinks he does hear his sister, the creak of small footsteps creeping tentatively up the stairs.

"Don't tell me to be quiet, you shithea—"

He puts his hand over Carrie's mouth. Carrie's super-pissed at that—she's clawing at his hand and maybe even trying to bite him so she can screech at him some more—but Evan thinks he hears another muffled step outside and presses harder to get her to shut up while he turns his head, listening, listening, for the sound of someone coming . . .

his hand
against my mouth
my nose

thrashed kicked bucked
forehead wet with sweat

his hand
binding and
burying the
narrowest last
bit of
air

I could not
breathe

*A*nd the air cracks.

  It's a noise, something between a rifle shot and a high-pitched cry. It doesn't come from Carrie. Carrie cannot speak; Evan glimpses her eyes, wild and panicked above his hand—his hand, which not only covers her mouth but presses up against her nose. He sees it all at once: his hand and her eyes at the same second that a noise like a cry is lost in the shatter of splintering glass.

I
could
not
breathe.

e lets go. There's a whooshing gasp as Carrie sucks in air, but in the same second he's off the bed, pulling on his jeans to run out the door, to the stair railing.

One of the stained-glass windows on the landing has shattered. The last shards are falling to the ground like shining bits of tinsel or snow, and in the middle of them is Libby, frozen in mid-step, eyes squeezed shut, slivers sprinkled over her hair and hunched, frightened shoulders.

I saw her under him.
When he finally rolled off,
she looked asleep.
Her pale braid, undone,
spilled across the crumpled sheet.

I watched him try to wake her,
give her shoulder a rough,
impatient shake.
But her head rolled, limp,
and came to rest at an odd angle.

I watched him lie there
next to her, his eyes wide,
his breath fast and frightened
in the dark.

The moon left a faint and
silvery gleam across the floor
as he padded to the doorway.

He looked into the empty hall,
then left the door open while
he went back to scoop her up.
Her arms flopped and dangled.

He carried her across the hall
to her own room.
The covers of her bed were
already pulled back.

He placed her on the sheets,
then tugged her nightgown down
to cover her legs.

Last of all,
he pulled the covers up to her chin,
as if she had been there all along
and nothing had ever,
ever happened.

He did not kiss her on the cheek.
He did not whisper any good-byes.
He did not pause for one last look.
He just eased himself
out of the room,
careful not to make a sound
when he shut the door

and
left
me
behind.

I
once
was flesh.

I once
had quick thoughts.

*I once
had dreams.*

"**S**hit," Evan says. *The floor of the landing is covered with sparkling glass.*

Libby opens her eyes and looks up at him. "I didn't do it," she tells Evan in a tight, frightened voice. Then she shivers.

"Don't move. I'm going to get some shoes on." He has to go into his room, where Carrie's going through the motions of getting dressed, but he doesn't speak to her—in seconds he's back in the hall, pulling his shirt over his head. Sockless, shoelaces flopping, he moves around the railing and comes carefully down the stairs, his feet crunching glass. "Are you all right?"

"I didn't touch it!" Libby breaks into sobs. "I didn't do anything! I wasn't going to come up, but—I heard—I heard a *noise!*"

"It's all right. You're not hurt?"

"I—I don't know."

"Okay. Just hold still." She doesn't look hurt. He squats down beside her and carefully starts brushing off broken glass, inspecting her for cuts. At the top of the stairs, he sees the open bedroom door shut, but he continues until all the splinters are off. Then he hoists Libby up and carries her to the top step. After he sets her down, he stops, he can't think what to do next: he's got an angry girlfriend in his room, a hopeless mess below him, and a sniffling sister clutching at his leg.

Carrie and the broken window are too overwhelming at the moment. He remembers the sound of her sucking in air—he didn't know that she couldn't breathe! And boy, she's bound to be pissed about it. He imagines he can feel her sulking fury radiating through the closed bedroom door.

He sinks down on the top step, next to Libby. And a moment later, Carrie opens the door.

She comes out calmly, completely dressed, every button buttoned. Her back is straight. She is not crying. Her face reveals nothing as she pauses beside Evan at the top of the stairs. "Is Libby all right?" she asks in an odd, flat voice.

"Yeah." Evan can't bring himself to meet her eyes. "I think so."

"Okay. Then I'm going to leave now. Good-bye, Evan," she says, and starts down the stairs. She is careful not to touch the railing, and picks a hesitant path through the glass.

He watches her, feeling that he should say something, that he has not behaved particularly well, but unable to think it out just now.

She's just past the landing when he speaks.

"Carrie?"

She pauses before looking up at him. Something in that pause makes Evan feel a little of what it costs her to maintain that level calm.

He's not angry at her anymore. All he feels is sad, and somewhat ashamed. They've been together a long time. And tonight—well, he knows he didn't do things right.

"I'm sorry." The moment he says it, he wants to cringe—he's really opened himself up now, she can let him have it for being a shithead and an asshole who dares to think that an apology even begins to make up for anything.

But for the first time today—the first time in a long time—Carrie surprises him. "You know what I was saying the other day, Evan?" she says, peering up at him. "About how I didn't know what I'd do without you?"

Evan nods.

"I guess it's time to find out, huh?"

And, with dignity, she makes her way down the glass-covered stairs and out of sight. Evan hears her footsteps across the wide, empty hall, and then the sound of the front door.

She's gone.

the front door

slams

the air is stirred

He *is the one*

left

behind.

ibby is quieting down now, with only an occasional sniff. She still leans against Evan; he puts an arm around her.

On the topmost step he sits,
clear and stark
his face is unfamiliar
his eyes are dark, not light,
his expression is
tired,
worried,
sad.

He pauses
lifts a hand
brushes one stray strand
of hair like cotton
from a small face.

it's not him

It's not.

Evan puts his head in his hands. He does not like sitting in the silence that Carrie has left behind. For a second he feels the weight of the quiet house; to him it is full of blame, regrets, and guilt.

He never meant to hurt anybody.

He doesn't realize that he's sighed until he hears Libby's voice, tentative and worried, at his shoulder.

"Evan?"

He raises his head. Below, on the landing, the fragments are beautiful, jagged and clear, amber and gold, orange and vermilion.

Evening sun
angles through the
shattered panes
flows down the steps

like

water

over

fall

leaves

faded light
on
old and broken glass:

the end
of
a

day.

elling Libby to stay where she is, Evan collects what he thinks is needed to clean up a large amount of glass: a broom, a dustpan, plastic bags, a trash can.

With Libby seated on the top step, watching, he sweeps up the mess.

Much later, after he has duct-taped black garbage bags into the window frame, Evan and Libby go into the TV room and he lets her pick the show. She wants to finish *The Lion King*. He's glad it isn't *Cinderella* or *Sleeping Beauty* or one of those fairy-tale romances.

On the couch, Libby leans against Evan's arm. He doesn't pull away, but lets her. She's holding one of her stuffed animals.

They're watching the part where the Lion King's father dies trying to rescue his son. Evan has always thought this part was pretty horrific for a kid, but Libby has never seemed to mind.

But tonight, when Simba is looking around the ravine for his missing parent, Libby asks a question.

"Evan," she says, "why doesn't Dad come see me?"

It's out of the blue. Evan has to think for a moment, to figure out how he can put it. "I think he's just kind of busy right now," he tells her. "Busy and mixed-up," he adds.

"What's he mixed-up about?"

"I don't know." Evan shifts uneasily on the couch. He wishes Libby had asked Mom about this, not him.

But Mom's not here. *He's* here, and he's the one who's got to sort it out.

"Sometimes," he tells Libby, "when people get mixed-up, they accidentally hurt other people's feelings." He has never really thought about this before, but now that he's said it, he feels he got it right, that what he said is real and true.

"But what do they get mixed-up about?"

He thinks again, picking his way carefully among the words. "About what they want," he finally tells her with certainty. "And what other people want."

Libby's frowning, unconvinced.

"Look," Evan says. "Lib. It's not your fault. You didn't do anything wrong. And you don't need to be the one stuck here feeling bad."

Her face clears—not completely, but a little. At any rate, she lets it go after that. They watch Simba heading into the desert alone, and are still watching TV when Mom comes home.

"Did Carrie come over?" she asks Evan.

"Yeah." Evan doesn't take his eyes off the TV.

"She didn't stay very long. Did she have to be somewhere?"

"Uh-huh." Evan's answers are noncommittal. He knows without looking that Mom has a sneaking suspicion something's not quite right, but can't put her finger on it.

"Did you have a nice visit?" she asks.

"Yeah," Evan lies. "It was good."

She nods and heads to her office to put her purse away. Any second, Evan knows, she's going to look up and see that one of her precious windows is gone. He waits, knowing that he's only got a few more seconds of quiet before another drama starts.

Mom's dismayed shriek cuts the air. He sighs. *Women.*

*The evening winds down, with Evan, Libby, and a still-*distressed Mom all going quietly about their business.

In his room at bedtime, Evan puts all the scattered papers back into the metal box. He doesn't bother to look at them. He vaguely feels that something is differ-ent, but it isn't till he's stowing the box on a closet shelf that he figures out that the hazy feeling of dread left over from his dreams has finally faded.

He shuts the closet door and looks around at the few beloved posters on the white walls, at the familiar win-dows now dark with night. The room doesn't seem strange or foreign anymore. He's been here long enough, he guesses, that it has finally become *his.*

He changes clothes, and as he climbs into bed, he thinks it's weird how he doesn't miss Carrie yet. He's pretty tired, but—at this moment—he doesn't feel sad, or lonely, or desperate, or guilty.

Right now, what he feels is *peaceful.*

I watch this one
slide slowly into sleep
bare, muscled shoulders

chest rises and falls

his breath
is shallow

quick

I never felt the knots
till they
unraveled

never saw the ties
till they
dropped loose

never knew that I was
clinging to debris
in someone else's wake.

He *has*
gone.

He *left*
long
ago.

This house

is

glass, wood, plaster,

tile, paper, concrete, iron

while

I

am only
a
whisper

and

an
echo.

And

all I ever had to do was

let

go.

I watch
this one's breathing grow
relaxed, deep

safe.

*Night
becomes
dawn
becomes
day.*

The front door
opens.
The air stirs.

I
roll like a wave
rise
to a crest

then
spread freely
dissolve around the edges

unfurl

into

the
light.